THE FIRST BOOK OF

TIME

THE FIRST BOOK OF TIME

JEANNE BENDICK

This edition published 2024 by Living Book Press
First published in 1963.

ISBN: 978-1-76153-436-2 (hardcover)
       978-1-76153-437-9 (softcover)

A catalogue record for this
book is available from the
National Library of Australia

THE FIRST BOOK OF TIME

JEANNE BENDICK

HOW DO YOU THINK ABOUT TIME?

How do you think about time?

Do you think of it simply as seconds and minutes—hours and days?

Do you think that time is something that never changes—that a minute is always a minute, and a year is always a year?

Janus, the Roman god of things beginning, had two faces. One looked back into the past; the other looked ahead into the future.

Do you think that the past has happened—and the present is now—and the future is ahead?

Do you think that there could be time if there were no people to measure it?

Now try thinking about these things.

Try thinking about the past, the present, and the future all happening at the same time.

Try thinking about time going much faster in one place than in another.

Try thinking about a clock that is alive. Try thinking about a clock that can measure a billion years, or four billion years.

Try thinking about a clock that can measure a millionth of a billionth of a billionth of a second.

Try thinking about time beginning, or ending.

Try thinking what the world would be like without time.

Could you imagine it?

WHAT IS TIME?

Everybody knows what time is.

But if someone asked you to explain it, what would you say?

Would you say that time is a way of measuring things?

Or is it a thing itself?

Would there be time even if we didn't measure it—even if there were no people to think about it?

We cannot touch time or see it or taste it or smell it. We cannot cut it up or add to it. We cannot stop it or start it, or turn it around and make it go the other way.

Did we merely invent time, because it's handy?

Or is it something real, like space?

We cannot see or touch or hear space, but we know it is real. All solid things in the world take up room in space. Things occupy space. They exist and move in it. We say space is a *dimension*.

People and things take up room in space.
They move through it.

Is time a dimension, too?

We can locate things in the dimension of space by asking the question, "Where?"

Can we locate them in the dimension of time by asking the question, "When?"

If you are beginning to feel mixed up because you cannot find the answers to something you always thought was simple, don't worry. More than fifteen hundred years ago St. Augustine said, "What is time? If nobody asks me, I know, but if I try to explain it, plainly I know not."

For thousands of years, philosophers and men of religion, mathematicians, physicists, geologists, astronomers, and many other people have been thinking and arguing about time. And they still are.

PAST, PRESENT, AND FUTURE

What *do* we know about time?

It doesn't start and stop. As far as we know, it has no beginning or ending. The scientific word for this condition is a continuum. Is time a *continuum*? We do not yet know.

More than two thousand years ago Aristotle, one of the greatest of the Greek scientists and thinkers, said, "Time is a continuous quantity. Time is not itself a movement, neither does it exist without change. *Now* is the link between past and future, but how long is now?"

Aristotle

St. Augustine

Seven hundred years later, St. Augustine wondered, "Does time exist? We can measure it, and we cannot measure what does not exist. But the past does not exist anymore, and the future does not exist yet, and how can we measure the present when it passes in an instant?"

One of the simplest ways we have of dividing time, in our minds, is into the *past*, the *present*, and the *future*.

The past is everything that has happened.

The future is all the time to come.

The present is right now.

But, in an instant, the present has become the past. The words you just read are in the past. In an instant, the future has become the present. Time passes. Can you say it moves?

Not exactly.

But we measure time by motion. We measure it by the regular motion of real things—the gears or pendulum of a clock, the flow of electricity, the ebb and flow of tides, the movement of the earth and the moon, the swing of stars across the sky.

Sir Isaac Newton remarked that we measure time by motion, and we measure motion by time.

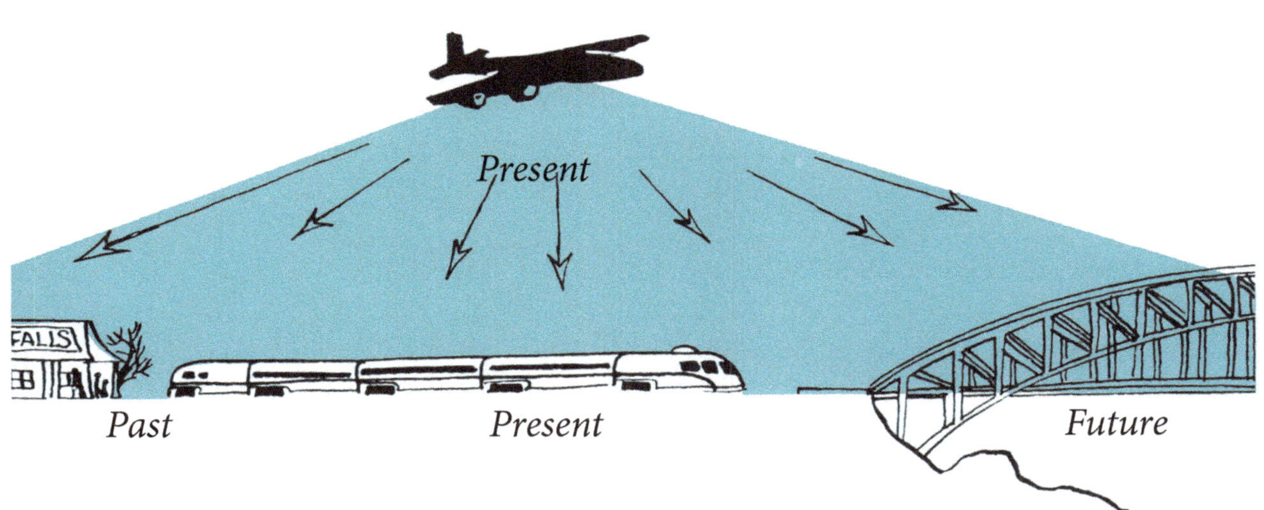

Are the past, the present, and the future the same for everyone? After all, the same instant is now. Suppose you are in an airplane, watching a train on the ground. To the people on the train, the station they have just left is the past, the bridge they are about to cross is the future. But you are seeing them all at the same moment. Your now is the past, the present, and the future of the people on the train.

MEASURING TIME

It was important for man to learn how to measure time. Everything depended on it.

Of course, it was important for him to know when it was going to be day or night—or winter, when the food was scarce—or summer, when the food was plentiful.

But most animals and most plants seem to be able to tell these things without having to think about measuring time. What else depended on it, for man?

Almost everything we know today.

Learning to measure time was the beginning of learning *order*, and all science depends on order. A person cannot even count without order.

When we say, ONE, TWO, THREE or FIRST, SECOND, THIRD what are we doing? We are putting numbers in order so that we can think about them one at a time. But we must have a place to begin. Something has to be first. First how? First in space. First in time.

So, learning the order of things was the beginning of science for man—learning that day follows night, that the seasons follow one another in a regular pattern, and that so do the ebb and flow of tides, that the moon is full and then full again after an exact number of days and nights. Man found order in the movements of the heavenly bodies, and they gave him his first ways of measuring time.

WHAT MAKES A YEAR

We can only measure time by motion. If nothing moved in the universe, would there be such a thing as time? Probably not. The scientist, Dr. Einstein, said that there is no such thing as *absolute* time—time by itself, with no relation to anything else.

But as long as there is motion there is time, and we can measure it. As long as a clock ticks or a heart beats or spring follows winter, we can measure time.

What would you say was our most important timekeeper, here on earth? You would probably agree that it is the earth itself.

As you know, the earth moves in several ways at once. It spins on its axis, like a top.

It circles the sun.

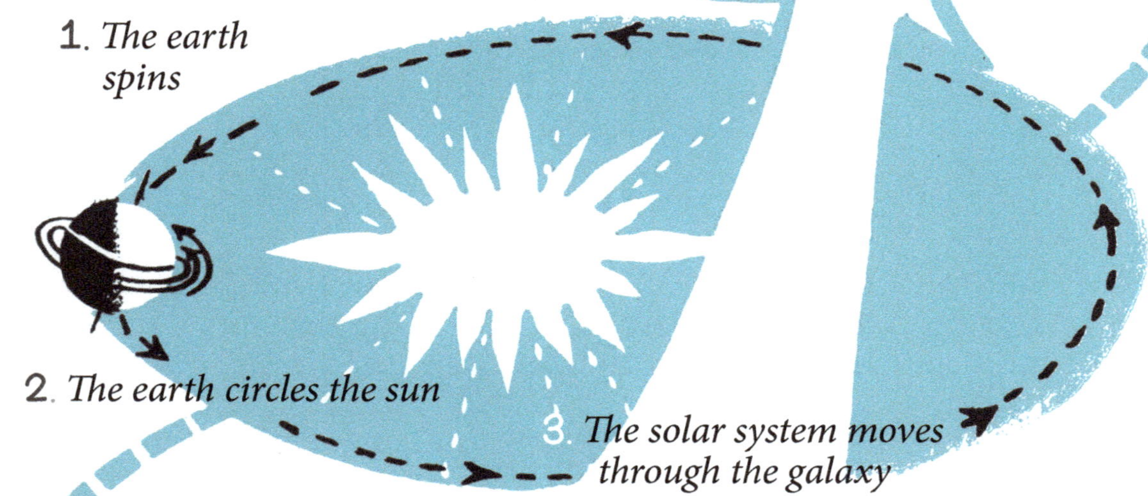

It moves, along with the sun and the other planets in our solar system, through our galaxy, the Milky Way. And, all the while, the galaxy itself is speeding through space, through the universe.

Which of these motions do we use in measuring time? Except to astronomers, nothing is evident to tell us about the motion of the earth through the galaxy and through space. But when the earth rotates on its axis, we can see that the result is night and day.

And when the earth has made a complete orbit around the sun, we notice it as a year.

The *solar year* (*solar* means "sun") is figured from the time the sun crosses the Equator in the spring, going from the Southern Hemisphere to the Northern Hemisphere, until it crosses the Equator the next year, going the same way again.

The scientific name for this time of crossing is the *vernal equinox*. Most of us call it simply "the first day of spring."

At the *autumnal equinox* the sun crosses the Equator again, going south, but the solar year is measured from one vernal equinox to the next.

The solar year is 365 days, 5 hours, 48 minutes, and 45.7 seconds long.

Another standard of time for a year is slightly different, but a little more exact. It is called the sidereal year. *Sidereal* means "determined by the stars." The sidereal year is the length of time it takes the earth to return to an exact place in its orbit in relation to the fixed stars—those stars which always seem to keep their same positions in relation to one another. The sidereal year is 20 minutes longer than the solar year.

Our *calendar year* is 365 days long. But what happens to that extra 5 hours, 48 minutes and 45.7 seconds—the difference between the solar and the calendar year? We save them up for four years and make an extra day of them—February 29. We call that fourth year a *leap year*.

A solar year is determined
by the sun

A sidereal year is determined
by the stars

A calendar year is determined by people

MONTHS AND WEEKS

What makes a month? The answer depends on what kind of month we are talking about. The months in our calendar were made by people. These months have no relation to the beautifully exact movement of the moon through the sky, which makes a *lunar month*. (*Lunar* means "moon.")

The lunar month is one of the three natural divisions of time. (The others are the solar year and the solar day.) A lunar month is the length of time from one new moon to the next. It is 29 days, 12 hours, 44 minutes, and 2.8 seconds long.

It starts when the positions of the earth, the moon, and the sun are like this—

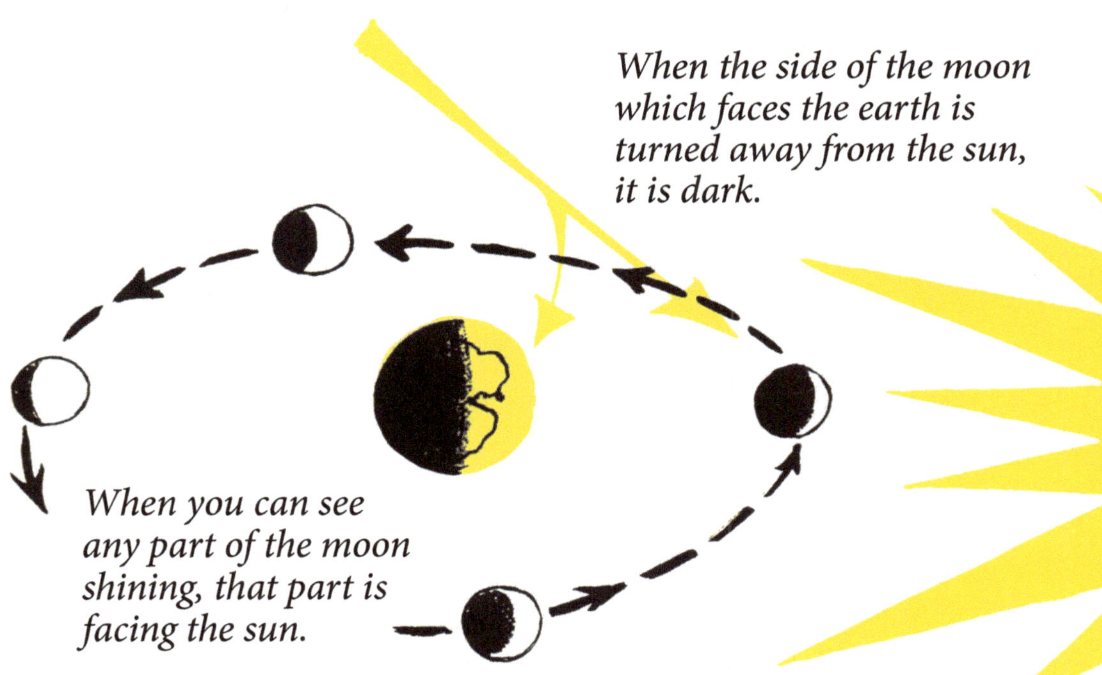

And when they reach those positions again, another month begins.

Sometimes a lunar month is called a *synodic* month.

Just as we use a sidereal year, we often use a *sidereal* month, which is figured from the time the moon is in conjunction with a certain star, until it moves into that exact relationship again. A sidereal month is shorter than a lunar month. It is 27 days, 7 hours, 43 minutes, and 11.5 seconds long.

Why don't we use lunar months or sidereal months instead of man-made months, and add them together to make a year?

Add 12 lunar months together,

or 12 sidereal months, and see what happens.

And a sideral month is even shorter!

WEEKS

Is a week a natural division of time?

Not really. It is a little uncertain how a week of seven days started, but it has been used for thousands of years. Except that it roughly divides the month into four convenient parts, there is no real reason for a seven-day week. The ancient Egyptians had a ten-day week, and so did the French after the French Revolution. The Romans had an eight-day week, and there have been four-day weeks, too.

Sunday is the sun's day.

Monday is the moon's day.

Tuesday is Mars' day. (The Saxons called Mars "Tiw"—hence, "Tiw's day.")

Wednesday is Mercury's day. (The French call it "mercredi"; the Saxons made it "Woden's day.")

Thursday is Jupiter's day. (The Saxons called Jupiter "Thor"—hence, "Thor's day.")

Friday is Venus' day. (The Saxons associated her with Frigg.)

Saturday is Saturn's day.

ALL KINDS OF DAYS

The first thing you probably noticed about time was that night always came at the end of your day, and morning always came after the night. This was certainly the first thing that primitive men noticed too, and their first way of measuring time must have been by days and nights.

What is a day?

A day is the length of time the earth takes to turn around once on its axis. A day is 24 hours. Part of a day is light, when your section of the earth is facing the sun; and part of it is dark, when your section of the earth is turned away from the sun.

The earth spins on its axis as it moves around the sun.

The 24 hours that it takes the earth to turn on its axis is called a solar day. Is there a *sidereal* day, too? Of course. It is about four minutes shorter than the *mean*, or "average," solar day of 24 hours.

When does a day begin? For primitive people it began at sunrise, and in some places it still does. In most of the civilized world a day begins at midnight. But midnight where? After all, the earth keeps turning, and it is always midnight somewhere.

If you look at a globe which represents the earth, you will see that it is divided, by lines running from the North Pole to the South Pole, like the sections of an orange. These lines are called *meridians*. Geographers invented them to help us locate immediately any spot on earth.

We'll talk more about meridians on page 28, but let's think about one particular meridian now. It is the 180th meridian, called the *international date line*.

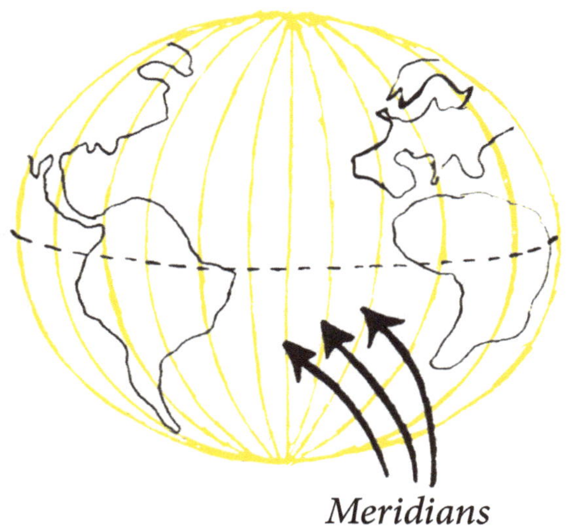

It is shown by the heavy line on the drawing.

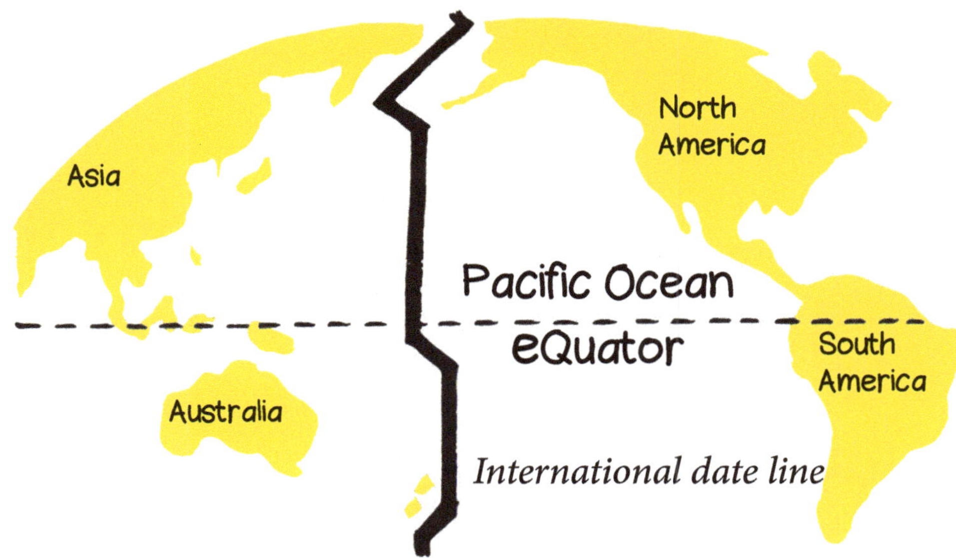

By international agreement, at exactly midnight along the international date line a day ends on the eastern side, and a new day begins on the western side.

Geographers picked this particular place because most of the 180th meridian runs through the open stretches of the Pacific Ocean. If the international date line ran through centers of population, things would be very mixed up. Tomorrow, or yesterday, might be just across the street.

You can see that the international date line has some bends in it. The line is bent so that all Siberia, and all the Aleutian Islands, and all the Fiji Islands will be in the same day at the same time.

Suppose you were on a ship, traveling west across the Pacific to Japan. What would happen when you crossed the date line?

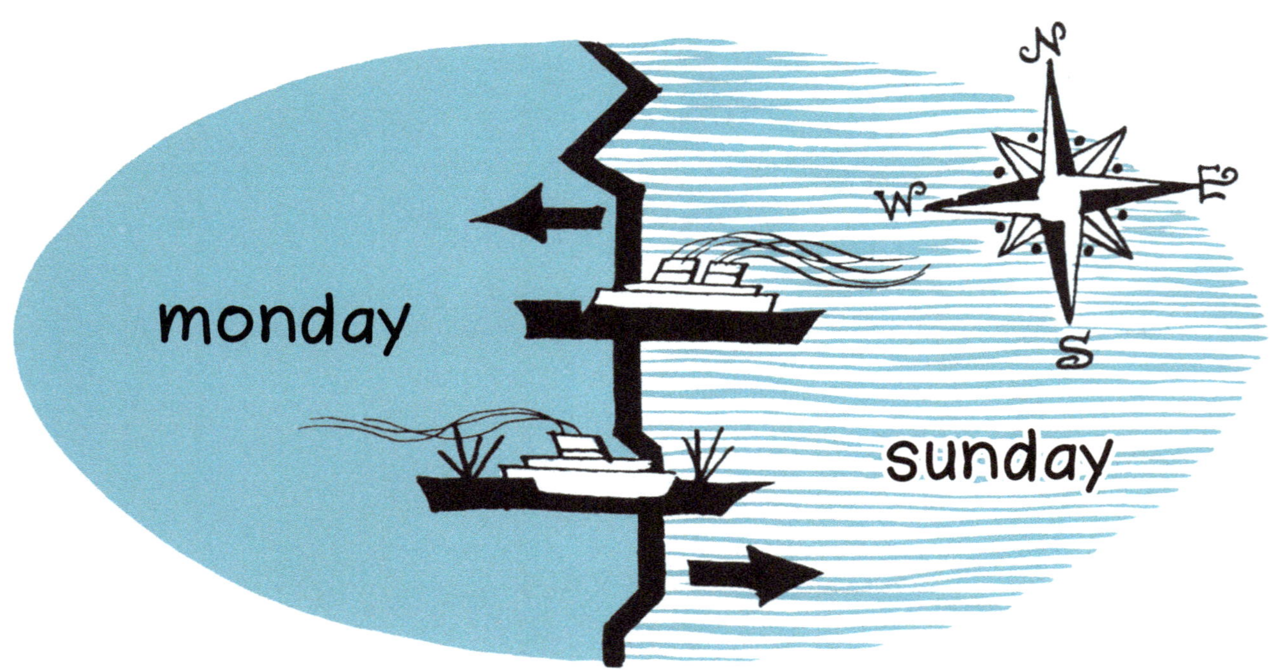

If it were Sunday, you would suddenly be in Monday. You would have lost a day. But if you were sailing east on Monday, when you crossed the date line you would be back in Sunday again. You would have gained a day.

Astronauts go back and forth, from today to tomorrow and then back to today, every time they circle the earth.

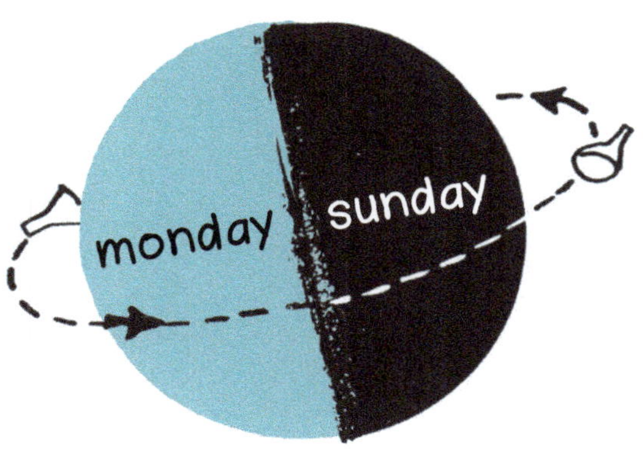

When man was first learning to measure time, he realized that during the winter months the nights were long and the days were short. In the summer there were only a few hours of darkness before it was light again. It was thousands of years before he figured out the mean, or average, day of 24 hours that we use now.

Only twice a year are the days and nights equal: when the sun crosses the Equator at the spring *equinox* (which means "equal night"), on about March 21, and again on about September 23, when it crosses at the autumnal equinox. At these times, the sunrise and sunset are twelve hours apart.

Now look at this. When the earth tilts in its orbit so that the North Pole faces the sun, it is daylight at that pole for six months, and dark at the South Pole, which is turned away from the sun. When the earth tilts the other way, it is dark at the North Pole, and daylight at the South Pole.

DAYLIGHT SAVING TIME

What is daylight saving time? Can we really save an hour of daylight, like money in the bank, to use when we need it? Of course not. The hours of sunlight and the hours of darkness stay just where they are. The only thing we can change is what the clock says.

If we want an extra hour of daylight to enjoy in the summer, we move the clock hands ahead an hour. Before we moved them, it was dark in the evening when the hands pointed to seven.

Now it is still light at seven, but dark when the hands point to eight. But we haven't gained an extra hour in the day. What happens early in the morning?

Before we set the hands ahead, it was light when they pointed to 5 A.M. Now they point to 6 A.M. when it gets light. That is why farmers do not like daylight saving time, and many of them do not use it. Cows and chickens do not tell time by clocks.

MEASURING HOURS, MINUTES, AND SECONDS

An hour is a twenty-fourth part of a mean solar day, but only because we say it is. An hour is not a natural division of time. It is only a convenience. *Hour* comes from a Greek word meaning simply "a time of day."

For many centuries, only the daylight was divided into hours, and there was a very good reason for that. Nobody could tell time at night, or even on a cloudy day.

Can you tell what time it is on this Roman sundial?

The first instrument that divided a day into hours was the sundial. The ancient Romans used the word "hour" to describe a particular time of day—the hour of sunrise, or sunset, or noon. The Romans divided the hours of daylight into five parts on their sundials. Earlier sundials had twelve hours.

In the seventh century there were
seven daylight hours, each named for a special prayer, and still the nights
had no hours at all. Nights were called "watches." Guards everywhere
were changed at the watches.

Even nowadays, time aboard ship is divided into six watches of four
hours each. A ship's day begins not at midnight but at noon, which is

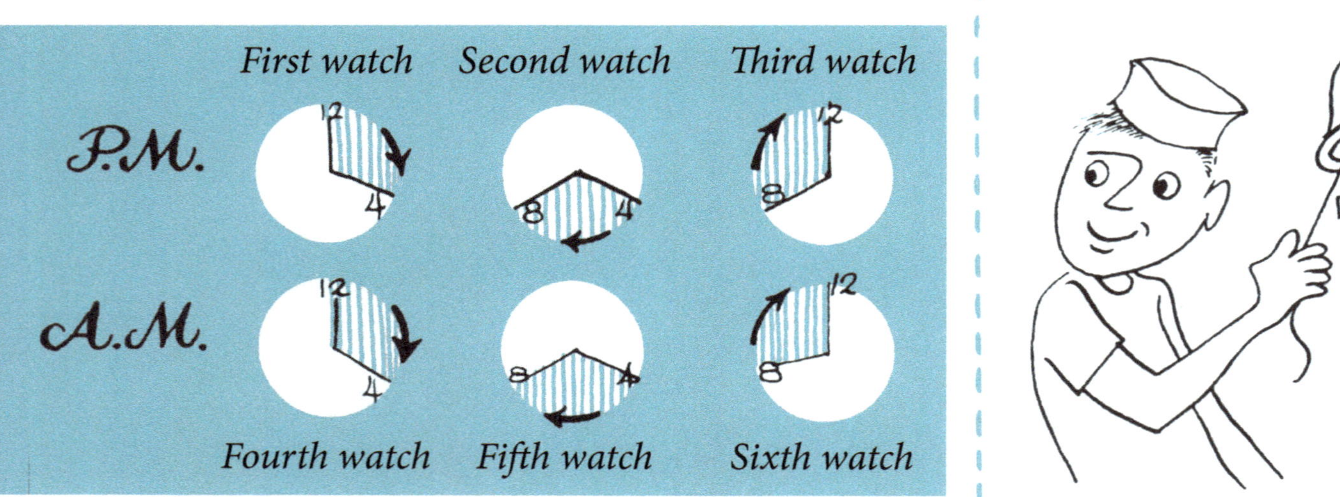

the first watch. A bell every half hour tells time aboard ship, from one
bell to eight, then starting over at the new watch.

When clocks were first invented they were not very accurate, and on
sunny days they were reset at noon. Because the sun is on the meridian
directly over our heads at noon, we call the hours before that time the
A.M., or *ante* (which means "before") *meridian* hours.

We call the hours after noon the P.M., or *post* (which means "after") *meridian* hours.

Because our day is divided into two twelve-hour periods, we use those letters A.M. and P.M. to avoid confusion. Otherwise, it might be difficult to know whether something happened at eight in the morning or eight in the evening.

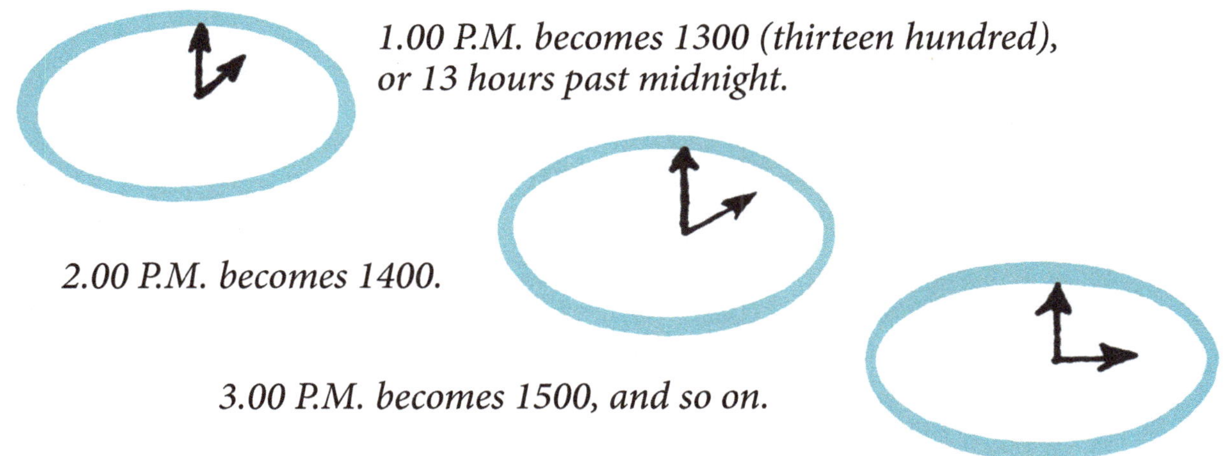

In some places the day goes straight through twenty-four hours, instead of being divided into two twelve-hour periods.

With this method no mistake can be made about the time. Military operations are always timed this way, so that there is no possibility of misunderstanding.

Before clocks became popular, people used to give the time as "four hours," or "six hours." Afterward they changed to "four, on the clock," or "four o'clock."

Does time have anything to do with distance? It must have, since it takes a day for the sun's light to make the 25,000-mile journey around the earth.

The distance around the earth—its circumference—is divided into sections called *degrees*. Each degree is marked by a meridian.

Like any circle, the earth's circumference is divided into 360 degrees, which may be written as 360°.

The earth turns 15° every hour, or 1° every four minutes of time.

Since it is not practical to have the time different at each of the 360 meridians, we divide the earth into 24 time zones of 15 degrees each. The time at the central meridian of each zone is accepted as the standard time throughout that zone.

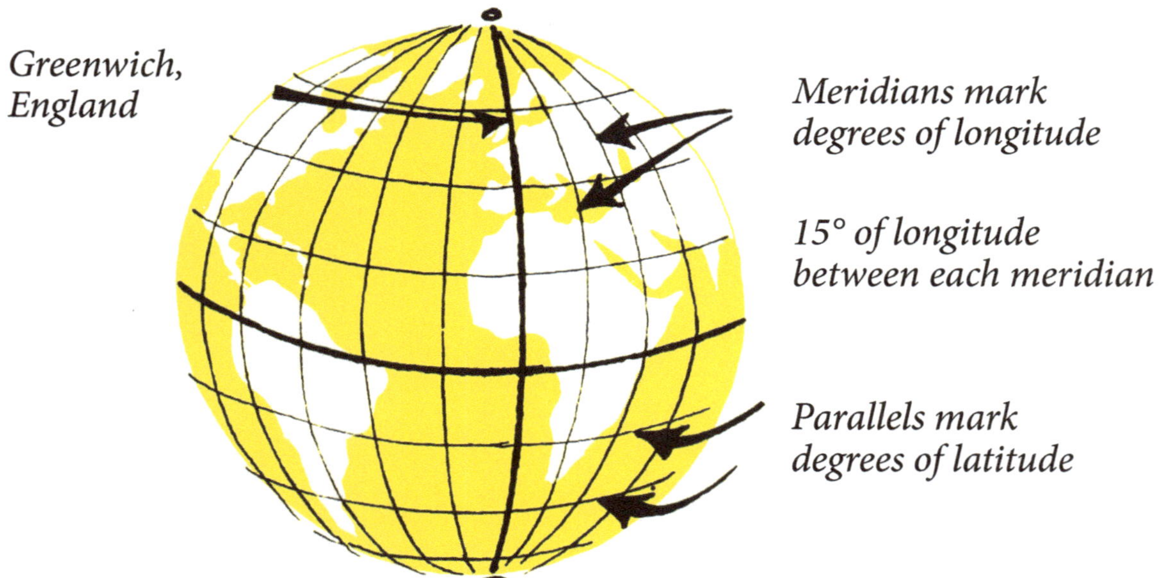

Time around the world is figured from the prime meridian, or 0 degrees, at Greenwich, England. When the sun is directly over this prime meridian, it is noon at Greenwich.

What time is it then, halfway around the world, on the 180th meridian? The difference is one-half of twenty-four, or twelve hours. At noon in Greenwich it is midnight on the international date line, and a new day is starting there.

The ancient Babylonians had a mathematical system based on division by 60, which we still use in working with circles—like the circle of the earth—or in dividing hours into minutes and seconds.

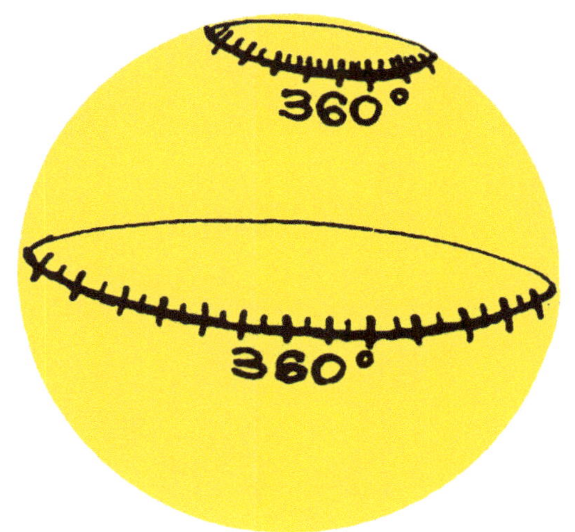

A degree of distance at the Equator is longer than at the poles. Points on the globe can be located by longitude, which tells the meridian, the minute, and the second, like this: 70° 40' 20"

The Babylonians invented minutes and seconds as a way of dividing circles—like the circle of the earth—into distance. Navigators still use minutes and seconds of distance. These, also called minutes and seconds of *arc*, are different from minutes and seconds of time. They divide each degree of the 360° circle of the earth into sixty minutes of distance, and each minute of distance into sixty seconds. At the Equator, a degree of distance is almost 70 miles. This gradually grows shorter, as the poles are approached, and so do minutes and seconds of distance.

In the thousands of years since the Babylonians worked these measurements out, nobody has ever improved on them.

SHORTER THAN SECONDS, LONGER THAN YEARS

Do we have clocks that measure anything shorter than a second? Certainly. Even in a race, the difference between winning and losing might be a tenth of a second, or less.

A tenth of a second seems almost nothing, because a second itself seems so short. But for some things a second is a long, long time.

A computer can handle eight million numerals in a second.

An electron tube can start and stop the flow of electricity millions of times in a second.

A television or radio station can broadcast millions and millions of radio waves in a second.

The atomic particles that make up a crystal of quartz vibrate billions of times in a second.

To scientists, a second can be a long time.

What is a long time to you?

A year goes fast. It isn't very long.

Ten years is longer—longer than many animals live. Ten years is called a *decade*.

Some animals, and some people, live to be a hundred or more. A hundred years is a century.

A century is not very long in history. The United States is not even two centuries old, but the history of some countries goes back thousands of years. The Egyptians were recording history more than six thousand years ago. A thousand years is called a *millennium*.

But a millennium is hardly a tick of time on the earth. Men have lived on earth for possibly a million years, but the earth itself is four and a half billion years old, or older. We call these great spans of time, which we cannot figure exactly, *eons*.

What is the greatest length of time we have an exact measurement for? It is a time and a distance both. We call it a *light-year*.

We sometimes call a stretch of time during which a particular series of events happened, or a particular material was used, an age. There was an Age of Reptiles, an Ice Age, a Stone Age, and we call our own time the Atomic Age.

A period that is marked by some new and definite order of things is sometimes called an era. There was an Era of Exploration and an Era of Colonization, a Steam Era, a Jazz Era, and more.

LIGHT-YEARS

How can anything be a time, and a distance too?

We have said that time is measured by motion. We measure a year by the motion of the earth around the sun. We can see an hour pass if we watch the hands move around the face of a clock. But what is motion?

Motion is a change of position
in the dimension of space.

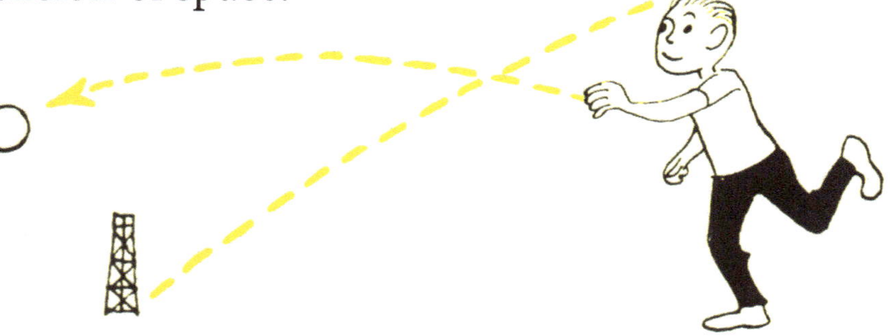

Everything in the universe is
in motion all the time—changing position. Some things move so fast, and over such unimaginably tiny distances, that we cannot see them move. No matter how long and hard we may stare at a wall or a stone, we cannot see the atoms in that wall or stone moving—even though they never stop.

Particles in an atom move at great speed. Radio waves move at great speed. They all can move as fast as the fastest thing we know—light.

Usually we don't think much about light moving.

When we look at a star, we are not seeing that star at all. It is much too far away. We are seeing the light from that star, which has moved across space from the star to our eyes.

Nothing moves faster than light. It travels at a speed of 186,281 miles a second. (To make figuring easier, we usually say 186,000 miles a second.)

In measuring vast distances, we use the speed of light instead of the speed of atomic particles or radio waves because those things *can* be slowed down. The speed of light does not change. It is constant.

A little arithmetic will tell how far light can travel in a year: 5,878,000,000,000 miles. A light-year is a unit of length equal to the distance that light can travel in a year.

Why do we need such an enormous measurement of time and distance? Because distances in the universe—between stars, between groups of stars—are too big even to imagine, and it would be inconvenient to measure them as we do everyday things. How could we measure, in miles or days or years, things that are *billions* of light-years apart?

We cannot really separate time from distance in space, or anywhere else. We cannot separate *when* from *where*, because neither one means anything by itself. (More about this on page 64.)

LEARNING TO MEASURE TIME

How did man first learn to measure time? All he had to do was notice. (And people are very good noticers.) Suppose there were no clocks. How many ways could we find to measure time?

We would certainly *notice* the difference between day and night. We might call the days *suns* and the nights *sleeps*, as the Indians did.

We would certainly notice how regularly the moon was full, then melted to new, then grew to full again. The Indians called a month a moon.

If we lived where the winters were cold and the summers warm, we could not help noticing that. We would see that the bare and snowy times and the warm and growing times followed one another regularly. Maybe we would count the years by *winters or summers*.

If we were very good noticers we would see that certain very bright stars or groups of stars were in different parts of the sky at certain times of the year.

If we lived by the sea we certainly would notice that every day, winter and summer, there were two high tides and two low tides, and maybe we would divide a day into *tides*.

If we lived by a great river we would see that at a certain time every year the water in the river rose and flowed over the countryside. Maybe we would measure time in *floods*.

During the day, good noticers would see that the shadow of a tree was long early in the morning, and grew shorter until it disappeared when the sun was directly overhead, then grew longer again, on the other side of the tree, as evening came. After a while they would be able to tell how far along the day was, by glancing at the tree's shadow—on a sunny day, of course.

Some of us might notice all these things, but how would we remember them? How could we tell when it was almost flood-time, or almost time to get ready for the cold? We would have to invent a *calendar*.

CALENDARS

A calendar is a system for measuring and recording the passage of time. Almost every civilization has had some kind of workable calendar.

People need a calendar so that they may prepare for things that are coming, and record events as they happen. How is it possible to record an event without a date? History would not mean very much if no one knew the order in which things happened.

But thousands of years ago, knowing what was going to happen was much more important than knowing what had happened.

The wisest men noticed the changing positions of the sun and the stars at different times of the year. They kept records until they could predict the seasons. Astronomy is probably the most ancient science because it was so necessary to man's survival. The astronomers, who were the calendar-keepers too, were powerful and important.

Even the earliest calendar-keepers knew that the solar year did not match the year of twelve lunar months, and they knew they would have to regulate their calendars in some way to keep them in step with the seasons.

In Babylonia, the astronomers added an extra month every two and two-thirds years, to straighten things out.

Many pyramids were instruments for measuring time.

The Egyptians were the first to use a calendar based on the sun instead of the moon. They began by starting their year when Sirius, the Dog Star, appeared on the horizon just before dawn, because this happened just before the flooding of the Nile River irrigated their farmlands.

The Egyptians' calendar was quite accurate. They figured their year as 365 days, and divided it into 12 months of 30 days each, adding the extra 5 days at the end of the year.

We know now that the year is about 365¼ days long. Slowly that one-quarter day the Egyptians did not add threw the calendar off.

The Roman calendar started in the spring too, in March. At first it was 10 months long. The Romans simply did not bother with the 60 winter days at the end of their year. Then a king added Januarius and Februarius at the end of the year because that gave him two more months for collecting extra taxes.

Julius Caesar

Januarius became January.
It has 31 days.
Februarius had 29 days.
Now, February has 28.
Martius, now March, has 31 days.
Aprilis, now April, has 30 days.
Maius, now May, has 31 days.
Junius, now June, has 30 days.
Quintilis, now July, has 31 days.
Sextilis, now August, has 31 days.
September has 30 days.
October has 31 days.
November has 30 days.
December has 31 days.

By 46 B.C. the calendar was so confused that Julius Caesar asked his astronomers to help him make a new one. They worked out a twelve-month year of 365 days, divided into months of 30 and 31 days except February, which had 29. They decided that, every four years, February should have 30 days—to account for the four extra one-quarter days.

And Caesar decided to start the new year on January 1.

The seventh month, Quintilis, was renamed July to honor Julius Caesar. Later, the Emperor Augustus renamed the following month in honor of himself, and took a day from February so that his month would be as long as Caesar's.

This Julian calendar was used for the next 1,500 years, but every year was 11 minutes and 14 seconds too long. Gradually, the seasons got out of step again.

In 1582 Pope Gregory XIII worked out the calendar we use now.

Years that can be divided by four are leap years, in which February has an extra day, to take care of the nearly ¼ day each year. But what about that extra 11 minutes and 14 seconds a year?

Tradition says that leap year is the girls' turn!

In the century years that cannot be divided by 400—like 1700, 1800, and 1900—there is no extra day in leap year. Sixteen hundred was the last century leap year, and 2000 will be the next. Now our calendar year is accurate to about 26 seconds of the solar year.

When did our calendar start?

In the sixth century, a monk, Dionysius Exiguus, figured out the year he thought Jesus Christ was born, and called that the year 1. After the date he added the letters A.D., which stood for *Anno Domini*, or "the Year of Our Lord." All dates since the year 1 have the letters A.D. before them.

Hannibal crossed the Alps.

Columbus discovered America.

All dates *before* that year are followed by the letters B.C., which stand for *Before* Christ.

B.C. years count *down* to the year 1. (Julius Caesar made his calendar in the year 46 B.C.)

A.D. years count *up* to the present and beyond.

Other calendars are based on different dates. The Jewish calendar starts on the date which tradition says was the year of Creation, 3,760 years and three months before Christ was born. The Jewish year starts in the autumn.

Mohammed

The people of the Arab world observe the Islamic calendar which began with Mohammed's flight from Mecca to Medina in A.D. 622. Because the Islamic year has only 354 days, New Year comes at a different time every year for 32½ years, when it has worked back to its starting point. The Islamic calendar is a very accurate lunar calendar.

The Maya Indians were good calendar-keepers. Their records of dates are called steles.

THE FIRST CLOCKS

Today's civilization would be impossible without clocks, but in the beginning, nobody could imagine measuring time as accurately as we do.

The earliest device for measuring time was a shadow-caster called a *gnomon*. If you know the height of a tree, it can be a gnomon. A rod, fixed upright, can be a gnomon. An obelisk can be a gnomon. The length of a gnomon's shadow shows, approximately, the time of day.

By the thirteenth century B.C. the Egyptians were using a sundial, and three thousand years later, sundials were still more accurate than most clocks.

A sundial has a gnomon, or *style*, which must be placed parallel to the poles of the earth, and a dial, usually horizontal, which is marked to show the hours of the day by the shadow of the style.

But suppose you wanted to tell time on a cloudy day, or indoors, or at night?

The Chaldeans and the Phoenicians, the Egyptians and the Chinese, all had water clocks almost as early as they had sundials. A clock that measures time by flowing liquid is called a *clepsydra*.

The first clepsydras worked like this. Water dripped from a cone-shaped bowl with a tiny hole in its base, into another bowl. The lines dividing the hours, however long they were, were marked off at different levels.

Clepsydra, Greek word for "water thief"

Greek astronomers used a clepsydra to measure the movements of the sun and moon, and Greek doctors used a clepsydra to time pulse rates. Some clepsydras were complicated. The Romans added a float containing a wheel which moved a needle, like a clock hand.

Clepsydras were used all through the Middle Ages.

An hourglass, with flowing sand, was a good way of telling how much time was passing, and people could carry these with them.

There were also candle clocks. Some were made to burn an hour. Some were marked off to indicate several equal hours

Hourglass

Candle clock

43

Almost anyone could make a gnomon, a sundial, a clepsydra, an hourglass, or a candle clock,

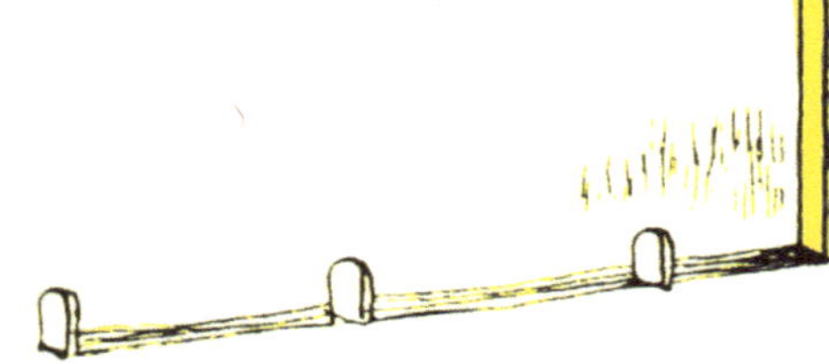

To make a gnomon, put a stick in a sunny place.

Put a marker at the end of its shadow at

8 A.M.

10 A.M.

2 P.M.

4 P.M.

6 P.M.

Would you need a marker for noon?

To make a clepsydra, you'll need

a glass jar or a soda glass holder, a large, cone-shaped paper cup (you can make it),

A glass to fit into the jar or holder

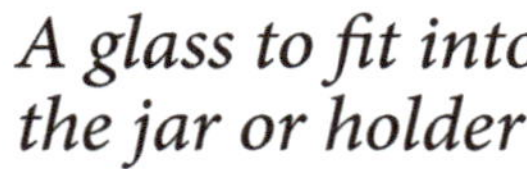

How long does it take the water to reach the first line? The next? What do you notice about this?

What help do you have that the ancient timekeepers didn't have?

Could you make an hourglass? A candle clock?

What would you need to help you?

But what would it take to make a mechanical clock?

The first mechanical clocks were made in the tenth or eleventh century. At the end of the thirteenth century there were at least two mechanical tower clocks in London. We still have drawings of a mechanical clock that Henry de Vick built in 1379 for the palace of Charles V of France. It had cogwheels, a dial, and an hour hand.

In 1581 Galileo discovered the idea of the pendulum.

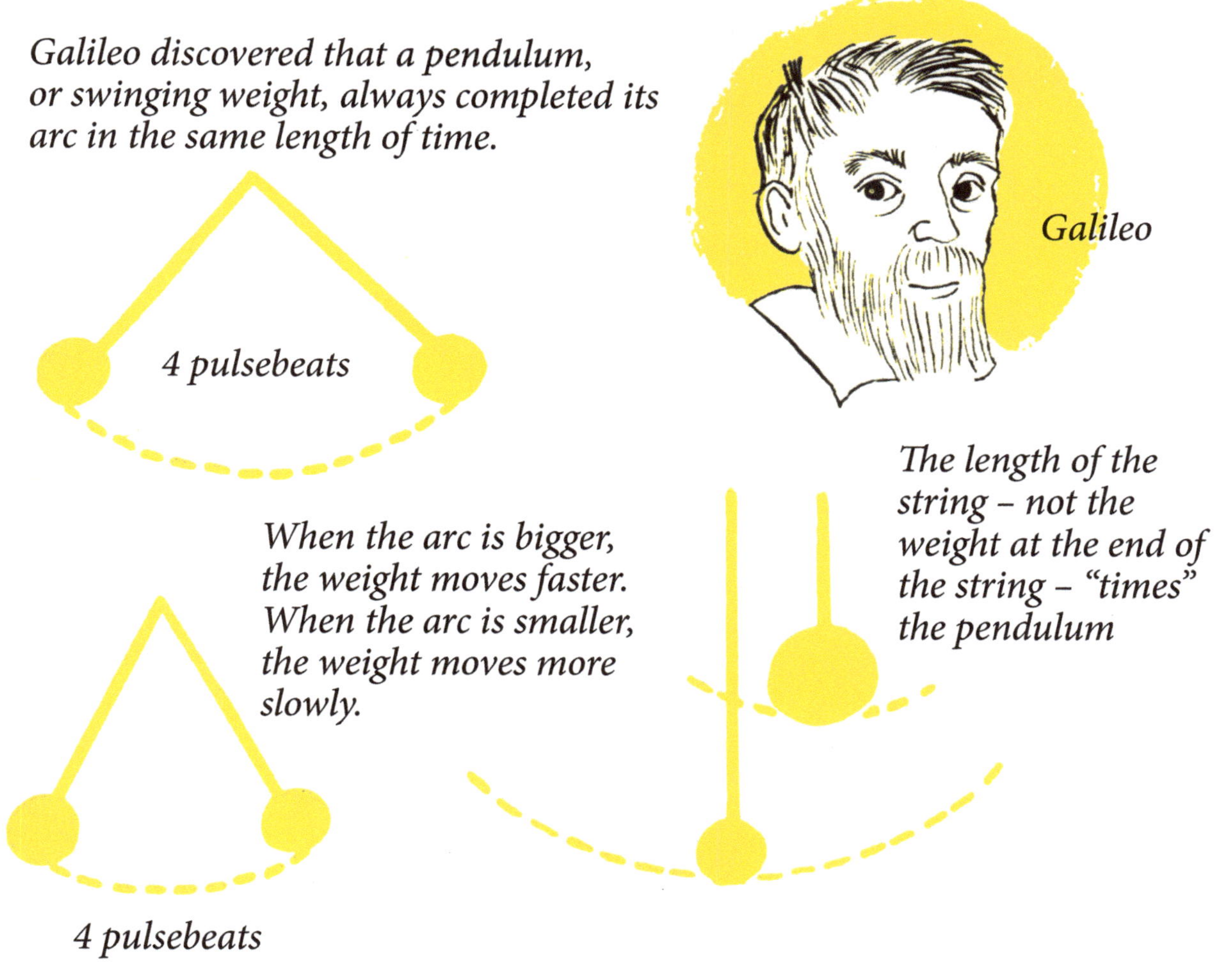

And in 1656 the Dutch physicist, Christian Huygens, began our modern, scientific measurement of time by perfecting the use of the pendulum to regulate the movement of clocks.

WHAT MAKES A CLOCK?

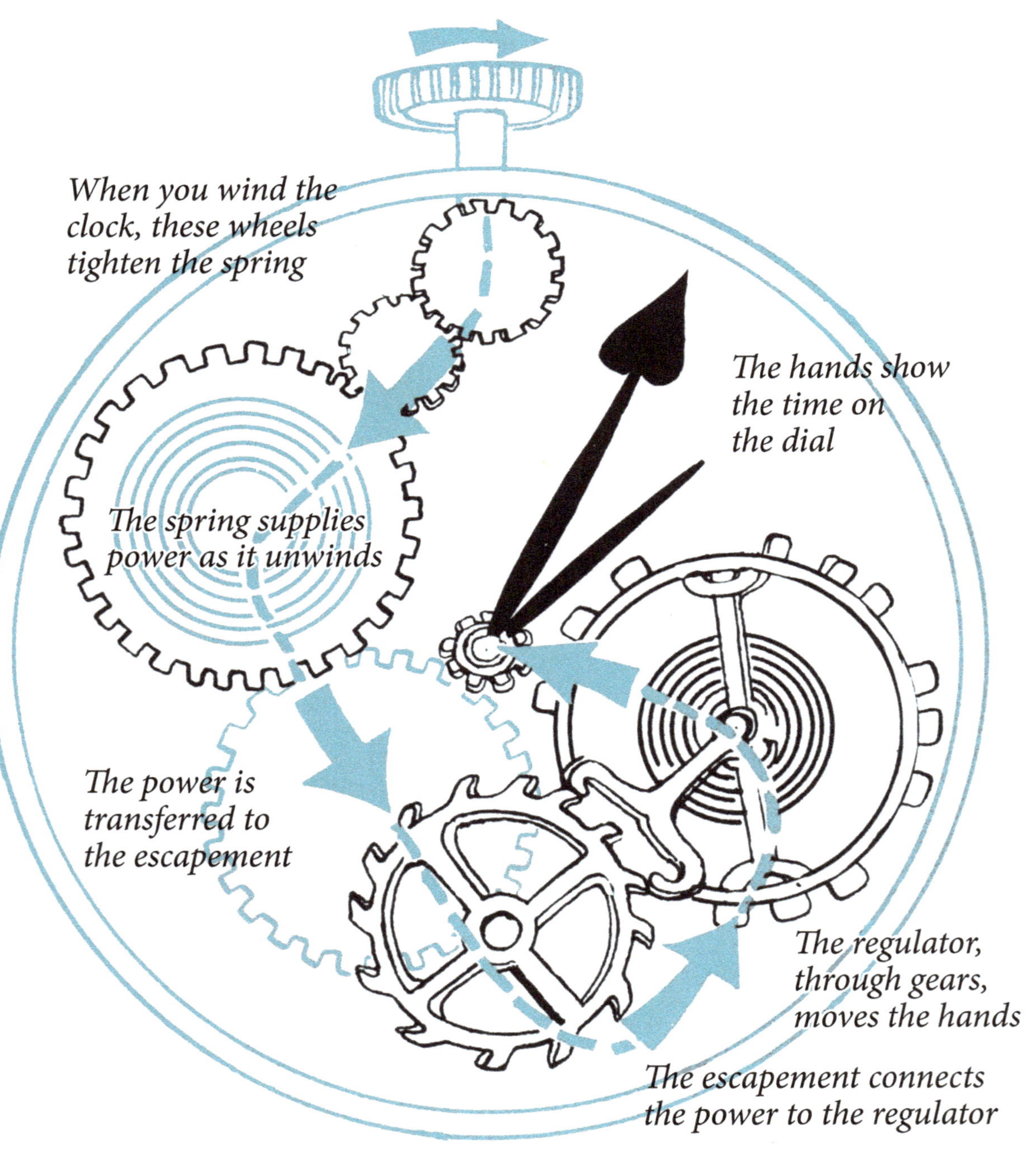

1. You must have a *power source*, something to make the clock run. It may be a weight, a spring, electricity, a change of temperature or pressure, light or motion.

2. You must have a *regulator.* The regulator divides time into equal periods like seconds, which can be added up into longer periods like minutes and hours. The regulator has to have a steady, regular movement. A movement like this is called an *oscillation.*

3. You must have an *escapement* to keep supplying energy to the regulator. The escapement connects the regulator to the power source. The escapement has a wheel which starts and stops. The wheel connects the continuous power from the power source to the regular motion of the regulator.

The escapement is the clock's counter. It counts the motions of the regulator and supplies it with power.

4. The *dial* shows what happens. It translates the movements of the escapement and the regulator into intervals of time marked off on the clockface so that you can read them. The clock's hands point to the time on the dial.

Some dials show only the hour and minute. They have no hands.

There are different ways to supply the power that runs a clock.

Winding some clocks tightens the spring, which supplies power as it uncoils.

Winding a pendulum clock winds a weight around a drum. As the weight falls, slowly, it supplies the power.

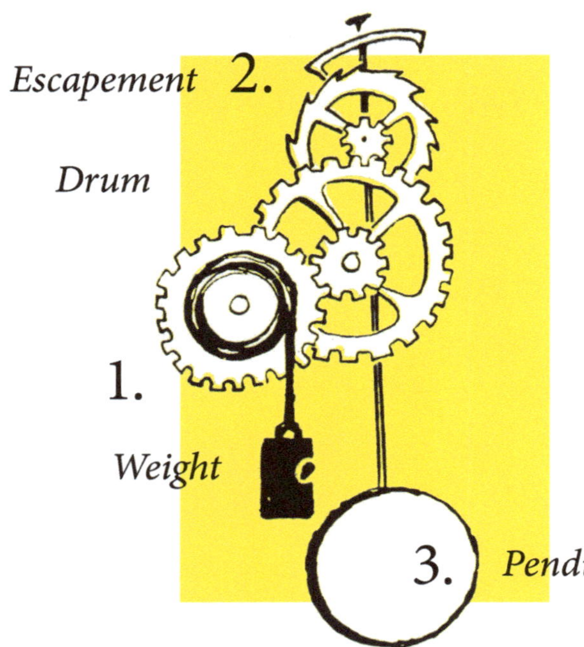

1. The power is produced by a falling weight, which turns the drum

2. The power is transferred, through gears, to the escapement

3. The pendulum is the regulator

It is not necessary to wind an electric clock at all, as long as it is plugged in to the current. It gets its power from an alternating current of electricity, which vibrates exactly 60 times a second.

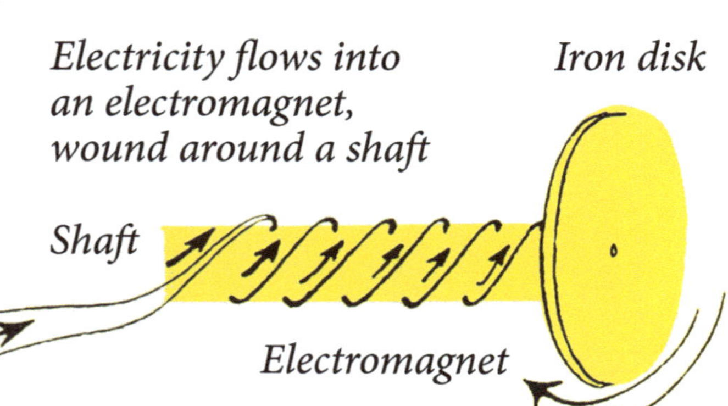

The current whirls the shaft, which spins the disk. The disk turns other wheels, which move the hands.

An electric clock is simple.

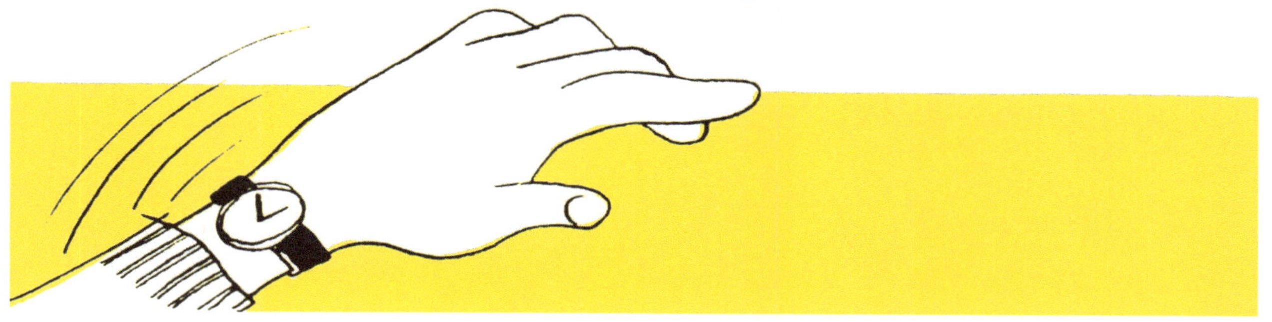

Some clocks, or watches, are called "self-winding." The movement of a person's arm supplies all the power the clock needs.

Sometimes the power is supplied by changes in temperature. Metal contracts, or pulls together, when it is cold, and expands, or spreads out, when it is warm. Special metals, extremely sensitive to heat and cold, are used in these clocks, so that even a slight change in temperature "winds" them.

The energy is supplied to some clocks by solar batteries, which are recharged by light.

All the clocks we have mentioned can be divided into two kinds.

Into one group go the hour-glass, the pendulum clock, the spring-balance clock.

These clocks are intrinsic clocks. Their timing device is inside them.

Into the other group go the sundial, the electric clock, the self-winding clock.

These are extrinsic clocks. They need something outside to help them keep time – the sun, electric current, the motion of your arm.

SPECIAL KINDS OF CLOCKS

CHRONOMETERS

Gimbals

All clocks are really chronometers. A chronometer is any instrument which measures time. (Chronos is the Greek word for "time," and meter means "measure.") But when we use the word "chronometer," we usually mean an instrument which measures time with exceptional accuracy.

All ships carry marine chronometers, which by measuring time help to determine the ship's position at sea.

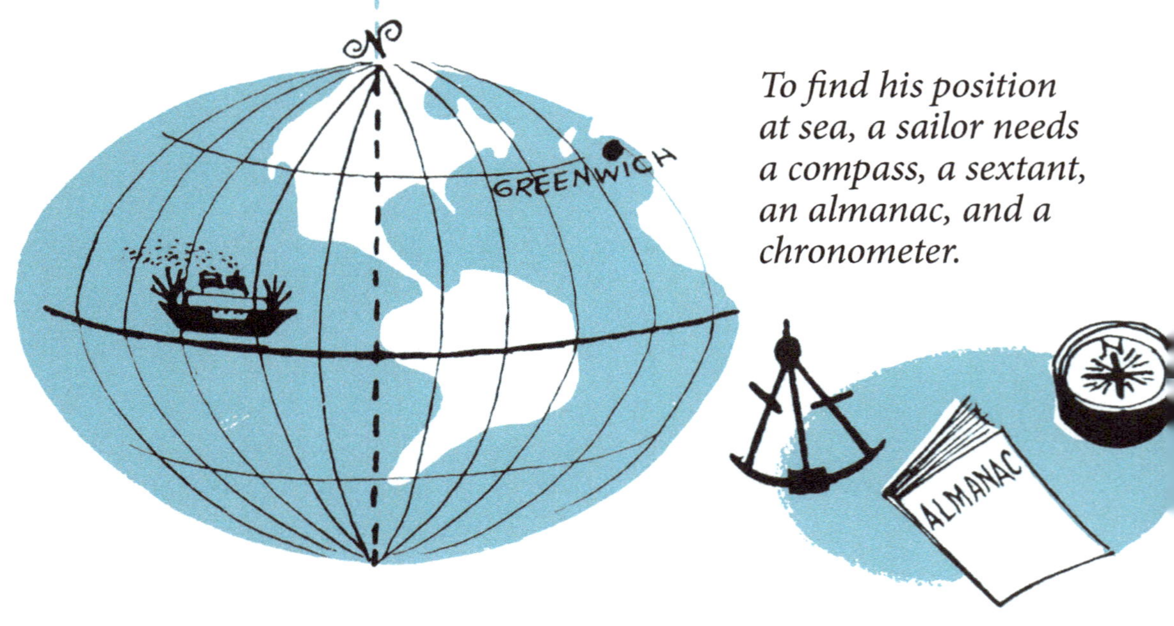

To find his position at sea, a sailor needs a compass, a sextant, an almanac, and a chronometer.

Chronometers on all the seas of the world are set to Greenwich time, because that is the international time standard. Chronometers are checked often against an official radio time signal that is broadcast all over the world.

A chronometer is a delicate instrument with more than a thousand parts. A ship's chronometer is hung in gimbals, which permit it to pivot and remain level even when its support is tipped. It is protected from dampness and vibration, from changes in temperature and air pressure.

Chronometers are accurate to within a second or two over a period of months, but there are clocks a million times more accurate than a chronometer.

ATOMIC CLOCKS

To measure time, an instrument must have some device, like a pendulum or a balance wheel, that repeats a motion, always in the same length of time.

The more frequent these regular movements are, the more accurately the timekeeper performs. You could say fairly that a fast-ticking clock keeps time better than a slow-ticking clock.

What is the fastest-ticking clock you can think of?

A pendulum is a slow oscillator (vibrator).

A coiled spring is faster.

Electric current is still faster.

But nothing oscillates—or vibrates—faster than the nucleus of an atom. When the nucleus of an atom vibrates, it radiates energy in the form of gamma rays.

Some pendulums oscillate once every second.

Some nuclei oscillate a million, million, million times a second.

A vibrating nucleus is a near-to-perfect pendulum. It will go on vibrating at exactly the same speed for a long time. No two man-made pendulums are exactly alike, but all nuclei of the same kind are identical.

And because an atom is shaped somewhat as the picture shows, the nucleus is protected by the electrons around it, and is not affected by changes in temperature or pressure.

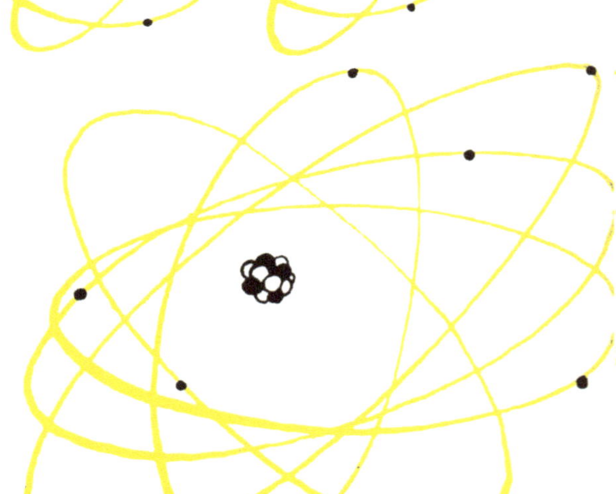

Whirling electrons make a wall around their nucleus

Of course, it is impossible to tell time by looking at the nucleus of an atom, since an atom itself is too small to be seen with even the most powerful microscope—and the size of a nucleus compares to that of an atom as a pinhead does to a parlor.

An atomic clock has a complicated arrangement of different kinds of nuclei releasing energy, which is amplified again and again by electron tubes. Finally, there is a special detector which acts as a dial.

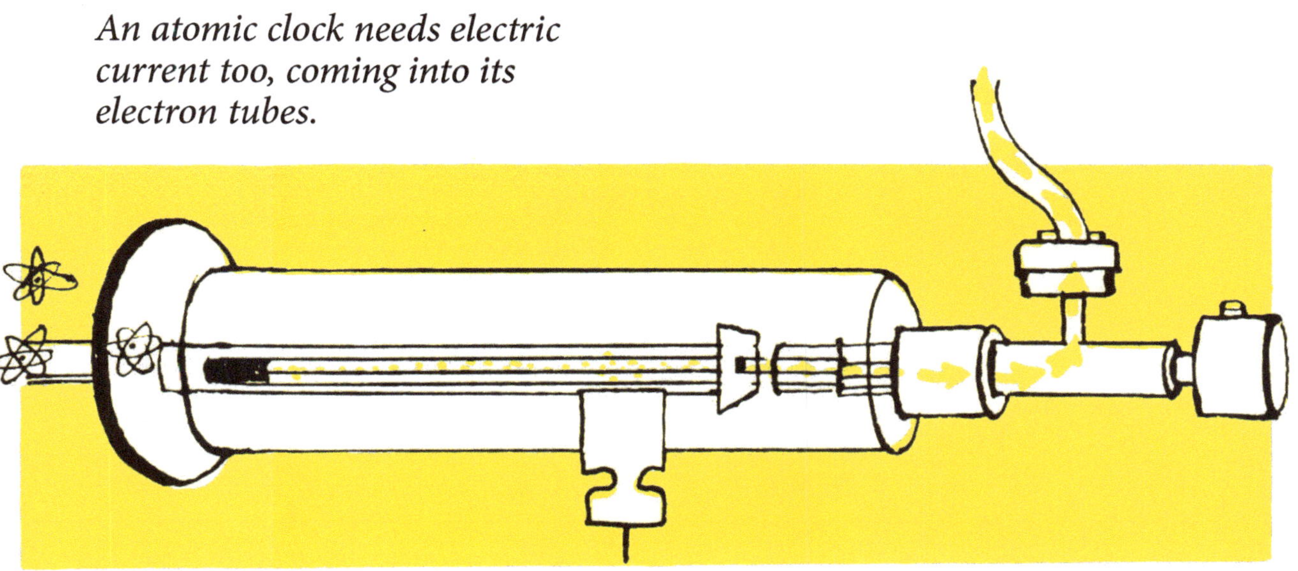

An atomic clock needs electric current too, coming into its electron tubes.

The unimaginably tiny oscillations from the nuclei are magnified over and over by electron tubes.

The time broadcast by the United States Naval Observatory is atomic clock time.

An atomic clock, with a hydrogen nucleus for a pendulum, keeps time accurately to within one second every 30 million years.

THE EARTH AS A CLOCK

The motions of the earth help us to tell time day by day and year by year. But the earth itself is a clock, which tells us about the times past, which are recorded on its surface. Scientists now think that the earth is about 4 1/2 billion years old.

Geologists, who study the formation of the earth itself, have many different ways of reading earth time. And just as we all can read not

	YEARS AGO	LIFE ON EARTH
CENOZOIC ERA	10,000-25,000	*Man everywhere*
	25,000—1,000,000	*Humans appeared. Large animals everywhere*
	12,000,000	*Many animals, like modern ones, on all continents*
	28,000,000	*Elephants came, apes appeared, redwoods grew*
	70,000,000	*Modern mammals*
MESOZOIC ERA	160,000,000	*Dinosaurs and reptiles, pinelike forests, flowering plants, dinosaurs died*
PALEOZOIC ERA	500,000,000	*Marine animals and fishlike creatures. Land plants appeared, first forests grew. Amphibians came, then reptiles and insects.*
PROTEROZOIC ERA	620,000,000	*Much simple life in the seas-plants, sponges, wormlike animals.*
ARCHEOZOIC ERA	1,420,000,000- 4 1/2 billion	*Sea plants, algae, one-celled organisms*

start here

only hours, but seconds too, on any good clock, geologists can break the larger periods of time on earth into shorter ones.

Time on earth is called geologic time. The earth's clock first begins far under our feet and comes up to the present—the ground directly beneath us. When geologists explore down through the clock of the earth, this is what they see.

The oldest time is at the bottom. The earth's story is recorded from the bottom up.

CHANGES ON EARTH	
Glaciers melted, climate grew warmer	
Glaciers in North America and Europe. Shores sank, mountains lifted	
Mountains rose, many volcanoes, climate grew cooler	CENOZOIC ERA
Rocky Mountains and Sierra Nevadas formed. Mild climate everywhere	
Mountains built up, worn down	
There were deserts and volcanoes, then swamps. Shallow seas covered much land. Climate warm and damp.	MESOZOIC ERA
Seas spread again and again over land, which was low. Thick coal beds formed in swamps. Land became higher and higher, water drained off, and there were deserts.	PALEOZOIC ERA
Thick sediments. Iron beds formed. Glaciers came, then lava. Sandstone and shale formed, and copper.	PROTEROZOIC ERA
Seas deepened. Iron ore and limestone formed. Mountains, and great formations of granite. Seas again, shale, limestone, gravel, mud.	ARCHEOZOIC ERA

Rocks are the calendar of the earth. Different kinds of rocks are laid one on another. Fossils—living things which were buried in rock or sand or mud—have left their prints of bones or shells for us to see. We can see footprints and raindrops, storms and ferns, seashells at the tops of mountains and tigers in tar pits. All these things help us to know what happened and when.

There are other helps, too.

Every living, growing thing on earth takes carbon 14 into itself in some way. Carbon 14 is an *isotope*, or an unusual type, of the element, carbon. Carbon 14 is *radioactive*: that is, it gives off radiations that are part of its nucleus.

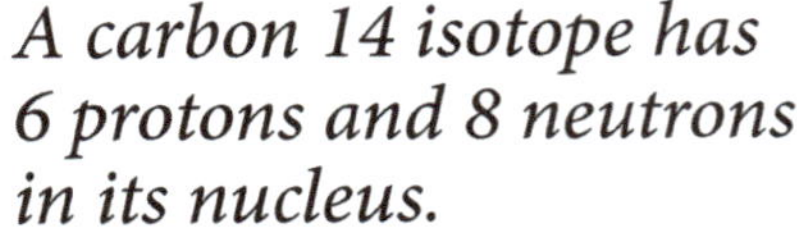

An ordinary atom of carbon has 6 protons and 6 neutrons in its nucleus.

A carbon 14 isotope has 6 protons and 8 neutrons in its nucleus.

The instant that life stops—when an animal dies, or a tree is chopped down—its carbon 14 begins to disappear.

Scientists have discovered an interesting thing about all radioactive isotopes. Because they radiate part of themselves away at a definite rate, in a certain period of time after the death of a living thing they are reduced to half. The *half-life* of carbon 14 is about 5,750 years. Anything

that was once alive would contain only half as much carbon 14, about 5,750 years after its death. In another 5,750 years there would be only half of *that* left.

Scientists know how many atoms of carbon 14 there are in the total atoms of any living thing. By measuring how much carbon 14 is left, they can tell how long ago a once-living thing died.

Carbon 14 is a clock that turns back time for about 50,000 years. While that is a short time in the history of the earth, it is a long time in the history of many once-living things.

Scientists have other ways of telling the past time.

Everything has magnetic force. And because the directions of magnetic force on earth have changed through the ages, scientists sometimes find "how old" by measuring the direction of an object's magnetic force.

It is also possible to measure the amount of heat and light radiated by anything that was once very hot, like lava, or pottery that has been fired.

And there are still other ways by which nature shows the age of living things.

The rings in a tree trunk show how old it is.

The ridges on a fish scale show how old it is, and so do lines on many shells.

Everything on earth has some kind of built-in clock.

If you look at fish scales through a magnifying glass, you can see the ridges.

PLANT AND ANIMAL CLOCKS

Rhythm is a part of nature. The planets move in rhythm around the sun—the moon around the earth. Tides and seasons come and go exactly. Everything keeps time, from the sun to the nucleus of an atom. Every plant and every animal is a kind of clock in itself.

Of all the living things on earth only man can tell time, but plants and animals do not have to look at clocks in order to know when certain things should be done.

Some jasmine opens only at night

Plants have regular times for making seeds and storing food and growing. All plants do this, not only plants that grow where there are warm, sunny summers and cold winters.

Some flowers are open only in the day, and some are open only at night. They close or open at the right times even if they are kept in constant light or darkness.

Day lilies close at night, even under lights.

Birds know exactly when to migrate and return.

All animals have built-in clocks of some kind.

Clams and oysters open and close with the tides, even if they are living in an aquarium. Crabs change color and move faster or slower at different times and tides, even if they are not near the sea.

Birds migrate and return on schedule.

Squirrels know when to store food. Hibernating animals know when to go to sleep and when to wake up.

How do plants and animals know these things?

Scientists used to think that plants and animals were intrinsic clocks—that all the clockworks were inside them. They experimented with plants and animals in sealed rooms, away from changes in light and temperature. They moved them thousands of miles, and still the clocks kept time.

And along with keeping time, some plants and animals do other interesting things, even when they are sealed away from their natural environments—the ways and places they usually live in. Some can predict changes in weather or air pressure a precise number of hours ahead of the change.

Scientists think now that the power source that regulates these living clocks is not inside them. Scientists think the clocks are regulated by the movements and magnetic forces of the sun, the moon, and the earth. There is no way for anything on earth to be disconnected from these power sources.

THE CLOCK IN YOUR BODY

Everything in your body has a rhythm. Everything keeps time.

You breathe a certain number of times a minute, and your heart beats a certain number of times. You blink and swallow as regularly as clockwork. Your body has certain regular changes in the course of a lunar month.

Even though you do not use it, because you have learned to depend on man-made clocks, you have a wonderful, built-in time sense. Most people can train themselves to use this sense.

Here is an experiment to try. Before you go to bed, tell yourself exactly what time you want to wake up. Repeat this a few times and for a few nights, and see what happens. Most people can be their own alarm clocks—but if you don't go off, it's no excuse for being late to school!

IS TIME THE SAME EVERYWHERE?

If you were standing on another planet, looking at your watch, a second would probably still be a second, and a minute would still be a minute. Remember, though, that the seconds and minutes and hours we use are man-made time, and not natural time. A day on earth—the time it takes the earth to rotate—is 24 man-made hours. Other planets rotate at different speeds. Only on Mars would the day be almost the same—24 hours and 37 minutes.

A day on Jupiter is 9 hours and 55 minutes.

A day on Saturn is 10 1/2 hours, and on Uranus it is 10 3/4 hours.

Neptune's day is 15 hours and 48 minutes long, and a day on Mercury is 88 times longer than an earth day.

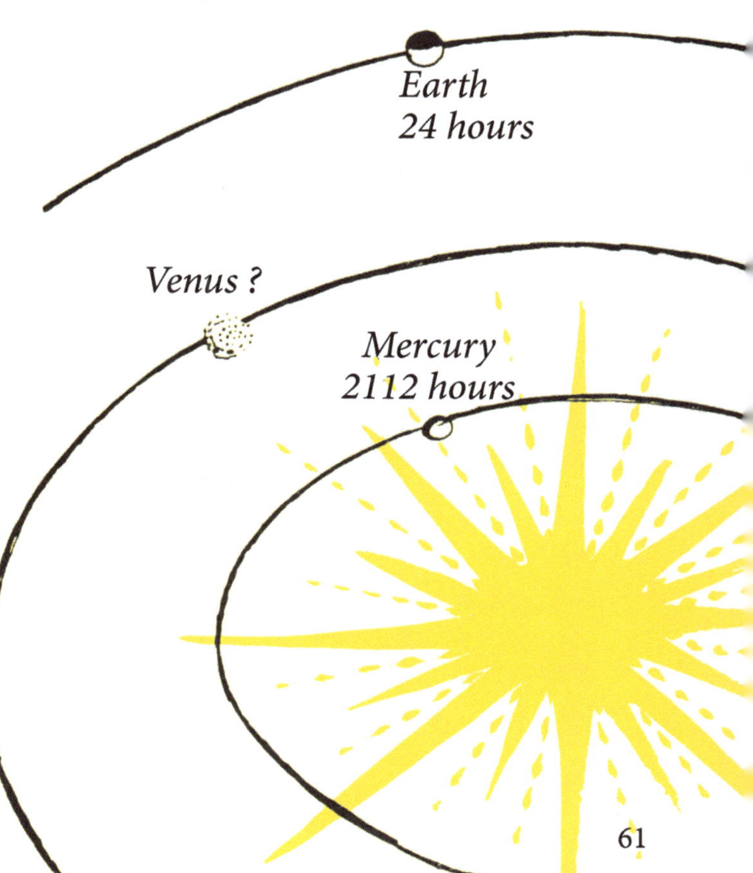

Scientists are not sure about Venus, because that planet is veiled in heavy clouds, but they think that a day on Venus is equal to 30 of ours. The length of Pluto's day is still a mystery.

Years are of different lengths, too, on the other planets. Planets with very big orbits take much longer than earth to travel around the sun. Planets that are closer to the sun than earth have much shorter distances to travel.

Suppose you were on a very fast spaceship, and you had a chronometer that kept perfect time. Could you depend on it to tell you earth time?

No. Time itself is not the same everywhere.

The faster anything moves, the slower time goes.

Dr. Albert Einstein

TIME AND DR. EINSTEIN

Almost everything we know in the world is relative.

We can only think about most things in relation to other things.

If we say, "The sun is very large," we are thinking of it in relation to ourselves, or the earth. If we think about the sun in relation to the universe, we must say, "The sun is very, very small."

A fly is tiny, relative to an elephant, but immense, relative to an atom.

A year is long, relative to a second, but short, relative to a century.

Things that are completely independent of other things, and not changed by their relation to anything else, are absolute.

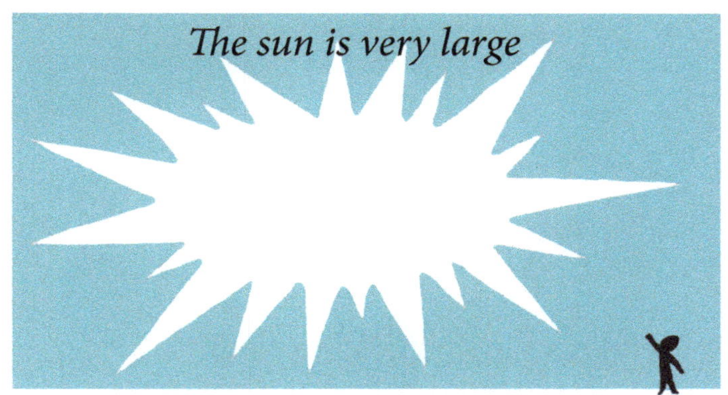

or very small.

People used to think that time was absolute.

They thought that nothing could change or alter the flow of time. A scientist, Dr. Albert Einstein, changed our way of thinking about time and about many other things, too.

The most wonderful thing about Dr. Einstein was not what he knew, but his way of thinking. His mind was free. He was not tied to the things men had always believed—even the things scientists had "proved." He "supposed" the most fantastic and impossible things.

Dr. Einstein's fantastic supposings led to his Theory of Relativity. By this he connected many things that people always had thought of as separate, into a pattern in which everything is related to the others, and cannot be separated.

Space cannot be separated from time.

Now has to mean **HERE**, too, because **NOW**, somewhere else, is quite different. Suppose, standing **HERE, NOW,** you see the flash of an exploding star. But the explosion happened **THERE**, a long time ago.

Every day, always, we combine space and time in everything.

If you have ever made a graph you know that the numbers going up the side, and the numbers across the bottom do not mean anything by themselves. The only important thing is the point where they meet.

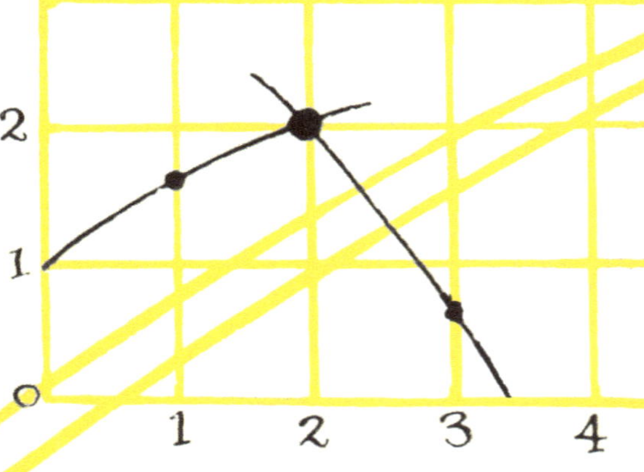

Dr. Einstein said: "It is neither the point in space nor the instant in time at which something happens that is real, but only the event itself."

The speed of light is another part of the idea of time.

The speed of light is absolute. It travels 186,281 miles a second, relative to everything. This speed is so constant that scientists everywhere write it simply as

c

c is the speed limit of the universe, as we know it. Nothing moves faster than light.

Dr. Einstein said that motion transforms things.

It shrinks moving objects into a different shape.

It shrinks the space through which they travel.

It slows down time.

Motion shrinks space

Motion changes shapes

Motion slows down time

He said that as speed increases, everything that changes with time—even time itself—is slowed.

If you were a spaceman, traveling 163,000 miles a second, time aboard your spaceship would go only half as fast as time on earth. For every half hour aboard the spaceship, an hour would pass on earth.

If your flight took a year, two years would have passed on earth, and you would come back to the earth's present, but into your future.

If you could fly at the speed of light, time would stand still.

At c, space shrinks to nothing and time stands still.

WILL TIME EVER END?

Time has many different faces.

When a person is worried or unhappy, an hour can seem like forever. When he is asleep, a night passes like an instant. And a happy summer can seem to pass like a day.

Time means different things in mathematics, in physics, in biology, in history, and in our minds.

Of all the living things on earth, only people can travel backward and forward in time. We can return to the past in our memories, and we can go into the future in our imaginations.

last year   *next year*

Do you know the word *eternity*?

For some people it means *infinite time*—all the time there ever is or was, time without beginning or end, time going on forever.

For some people it means *time-lessness*—absolute time, time not related to space or motion, time itself, by itself.

Some people think that time is an eternity, with no beginning or end, reaching into forever.

Some people think that time will last only as long as there are creatures to measure it and to place things in it, and that time by itself, like numbers with no one to count them, would be nothing.

Some people think that time will last until the last thing in the universe has stopped moving—until every star and moon and planet has fallen to dust, until every atom has stopped vibrating.

What do you think?

9 781761 534379